nickelodeon

ni hao, kai-lan

Princess
Kai-lan

adapted by Diana Michaels

based on the screenplay written by Chris Nee and Sascha Paladino

illustrated by Kellee Riley

Ready-to-Read

SIMON SPOTLIGHT/NICKELODEON
New York   London   Toronto   Sydney

Based on the TV series *Ni Hao, Kai-lan!*™ as seen on Nick Jr.™

SIMON SPOTLIGHT/NICKELODEON
An imprint of Simon & Schuster Children's Publishing Division
1230 Avenue of the Americas, New York, New York 10020
© 2010 Viacom International Inc. All Rights Reserved. NICKELODEON, *Ni Hao, Kai-lan!*,
and all related titles, logos and characters are trademarks of Viacom International Inc.
All rights reserved, including the right of reproduction in whole or in part in any form.
SIMON SPOTLIGHT, READY-TO-READ, and colophon are registered trademarks of Simon & Schuster, Inc.
For information about special discounts for bulk purchases, please contact Simon & Schuster Special Sales at
1-866-506-1949 or business@simonandschuster.com.
Manufactured in the United States of America 0710 LAK
First Edition
2 4 6 8 10 9 7 5 3 1
ISBN 978-1-4424-0351-2

Ni hao! I am .

KAI-LAN

I am playing BUTTERFLY BALL with

my friends TOLEE, RINTOO, and HOHO.

Look! Something in the sky

is flying this way!

Look! It landed near a .
TREE

It is the  !
MONKEY KING

He needs our help.

He will use his magic
STICK

to show us what is wrong.

"A  divides the two

WALL

KINGDOMS

in the Land of FOXES and BEARS.

The FOXES and the BEARS are not

friends," says the MONKEY KING.

The  needs our help

MONKEY KING

to show the 🐻🐻 and the 🦊🦊

BEARS   FOXES

how to be friends.

Will we help the 🐒 ?

MONKEY KING

Of course! Friends always

help friends!

Tiao! Jump!

We jump onto  that
CLOUDS
take us to the Land of
FOXES
and .
BEARS

We made it to the Land of

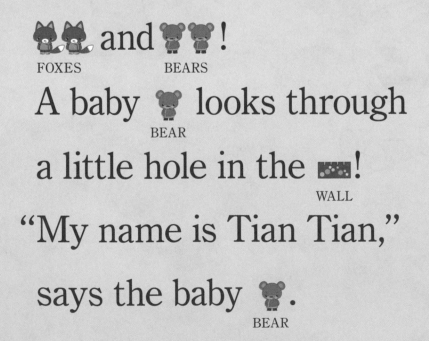 and 🐻🐻!

FOXES   BEARS

A baby 🐻 looks through

BEAR

a little hole in the 🧱!

WALL

"My name is Tian Tian,"

says the baby 🐻.

BEAR

Then a baby  says hello.
FOX

"I am Xin Xin," he says.

"Would you like a 🍑?"
PEACH

I want a 🍑! So do 🐵, 🐨,
PEACH   HOHO   TOLEE

and 🐯!
RINTOO

"I want a  too, !" says
PEACH   KAI-LAN
Tian Tian.

"Can you ask the baby for
FOX
me? do not speak to ."
BEARS   FOXES
I ask Tian Tian to try.

The baby  gives a 🍑 to
FOX   PEACH
the baby 🐻!
BEAR
Now they are friends!
If the 👑🐻 and 👑🦊 talk,
BEAR QUEEN   FOX KING
maybe they could be
friends too!

First we will talk to the .
FOX KING

I see a ! Do you see it?
CASTLE

That is where the  lives.
FOX KING

The  are locked.
CASTLE DOORS

We need to talk to the 🦊.
FOX KING

We will find a way to sneak

inside!

Be very quiet!

The  does not want to talk to us.

FOX KING

But I have a 🎁 for him.

PRESENT

I brought him a 🍑.

PEACH

The  likes the 🍑.
FOX KING   PEACH

Now he will talk to us!

He explains why the 🦊🦊
FOXES

and the 🐻🐻 are not friends.
BEARS

"We are not friends with
the 🐻🐻 because they
BEARS
make the 🌿 shake when
GROUND
they dance," says the 🦊 .
FOX KING
"The shaking makes us mad."

The  never told the
FOXES   BEARS
why they are mad.

So the might not know!
BEARS
We must talk to the
BEAR QUEEN

"Why are the 🐻🐻 mad at the
BEARS

🦊🦊?" we ask the 👑.
FOXES   BEAR QUEEN

"Their singing is too loud,"

says the 👑.
BEAR QUEEN

"It makes us mad."

I know how we can help!
When you feel mad,
talk about what is making
you mad, so your friends
can help you like good
friends do!

The  and the

talk to each other!
If they talk about what is
wrong, maybe they can
become friends!

"Oh! We did not know our dancing makes you angry," says the  .

BEAR QUEEN

"And we did not know our singing bothers you," says the  . "We are sorry."

FOX KING

The says,
BEAR QUEEN
"The can dance
BEARS
and the can sing at
FOXES
the same time!
We will all be friends and
play together!"

The 🦊, and 🐻 say,

FOX KING BEAR QUEEN

"We will take down the 🧱,

WALL

and make this a 🏯 of

KINGDOM

Friends. 👧 will be our

KAI-LAN

princess! Princess 👧!

KAI-LAN

Princess of Friends!"

So the  start singing,
FOXES

and the  start dancing.
BEARS

It is a party!

They are all friends!